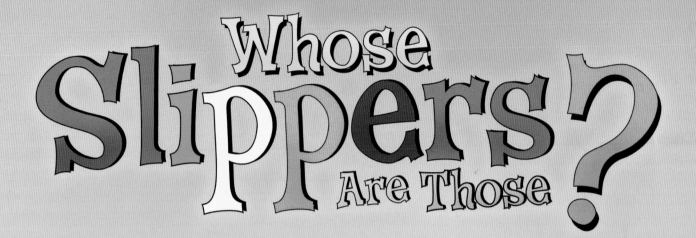

Whose Slippers Are Those?

Written by
Marilyn Kahalewai

Illustrated by
Gavin Kobayashi

3565 Harding Avenue • Honolulu, Hawai'i 96816
Toll Free: (800) 910-2377 • Phone: (808) 734-7159 • Fax: (808) 732-3627
Email: info@besspress.com • Website: www.besspress.com

Library of Congress Cataloging-in-Publication Data

Kahalewai, Marilyn.
  Whose slippers are those? /
Marilyn Kahalewai ; illustrated by
Gavin Kobayashi.
     p.   cm.
  Includes illustrations.
  ISBN 1-57306-238-3
  1. Thongs (Sandals) - Hawaii -
Juvenile literature. 2. Footwear -
Hawaii - Juvenile literature.
3. Shoes - Hawaii - Juvenile
literature. I. Kobayashi, Gavin.
II. Title.
TS1020.K34 2005   [E]-dc21

Printed by Sun Fung Offset Binding Co., Ltd., in China

In loving memory of Marilyn Kahalewai

And for Melanie Kobayashi, who always
enjoys watching her daughter Hunter-Logan play with slippers

red slippers

blue slippers

old slippers

new slippers

great big fat slippers

skinny little flat slippers

pretty, shiny black slippers

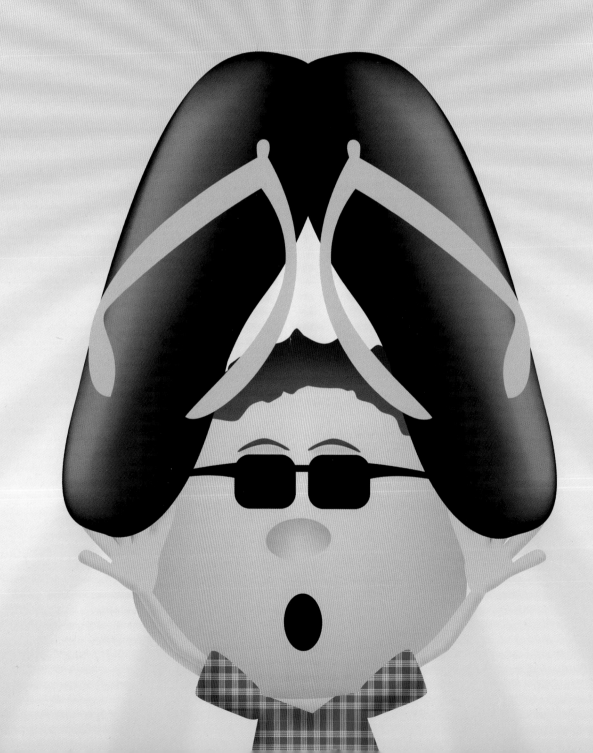

strap-around-the-back slippers

yellow slippers   green slippers

muddy slippers

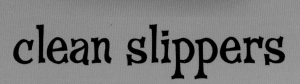

clean slippers

broken slippers

fixed slippers

same slippers

mixed slippers

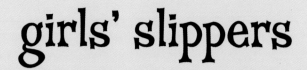

girls' slippers

boys' slippers

wood
slippers

painted
slippers

straw
slippers

Who gets to wear slippers?

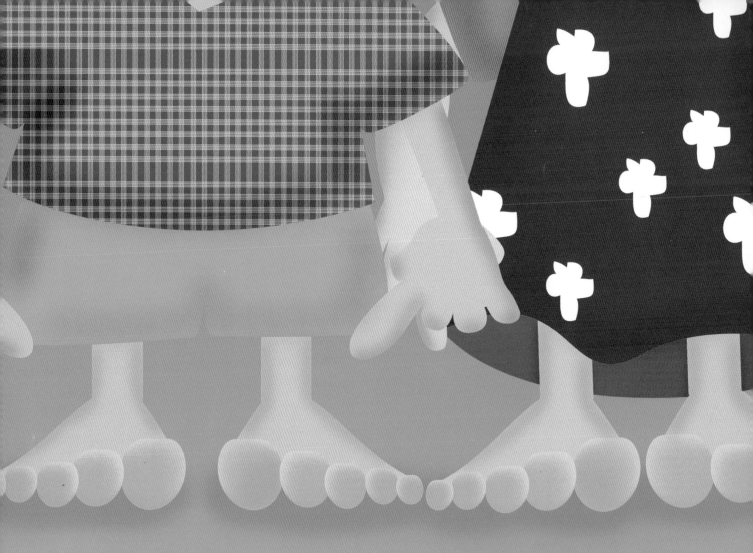

Feet!